PUFFIN BOOKS

LiZZiE & LUCKY

The Mystery of the
Missing Puppies

Megan Rix is the hugely popular author of animal adventure books set in the modern day and key periods of history. An animal advocate and dog-friend, Megan draws inspiration from her own adorable dogs Traffy, Bella, Freya and Ellie.

Follow Megan Rix on Twitter
@megan_rix
#LizzieandLucky

Books by Megan Rix

THE GREAT FIRE DOGS

THE BOMBER DOG

THE GREAT ESCAPE

THE VICTORY DOGS

A SOLDIER'S FRIEND

THE RUNAWAYS

ECHO COME HOME

THE HERO PUP

THE PAW HOUSE

THE LOST WAR DOG

For younger readers

ROSA AND THE DARING DOG

WINSTON AND THE MARMALADE CAT

EMMELINE AND THE PLUCKY PUP

FLORENCE AND THE MISCHIEVOUS KITTEN

LiZZiE & LUCKY

The Mystery of the Missing Puppies

Megan Rix

Illustrated by Tim Budgen

PUFFIN

PUFFIN BOOKS

UK | USA | Canada | Ireland | Australia
India | New Zealand | South Africa

Puffin is part of the Penguin Random House group of companies
whose addresses can be found at global.penguinrandomhouse.com.

www.penguin.co.uk
www.puffin.co.uk
www.ladybird.co.uk

First published 2020

001

Text copyright © Megan Rix, 2020
Illustrations by Tim Budgen
The moral right of the author has been asserted

Set in Bembo MT Std
Text design by Mandy Norman
Printed in Great Britain by Clays Ltd, Elcograf S.p.A.

The authorized representative in the EEA is Penguin Random House Ireland,
Morrison Chambers, 32 Nassau Street, Dublin D02 YH68

A CIP catalogue record for this book is available from the British Library

ISBN: 978–0–241–45551–7

All correspondence to:
Puffin Books
Penguin Random House Children's, One Embassy Gardens
8 Viaduct Gardens, London SW11 7BW

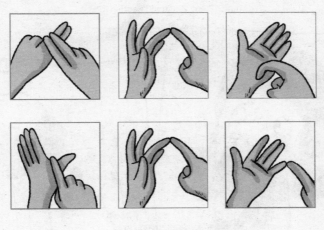

– M.R.

With thanks to:
Julia, Alfie and Baxter the wonder dog! x
– T.B.

WHO'S WHO

Lizzie

Lucky

Ted

Dad

Mum

Mrs Samuels

CHAPTER 1

'How's your list going?' Lizzie's best friend, Ted, signed to her on Saturday morning. They were in Ted's back garden cleaning out Thumper and Wriggles's hutch. Lizzie had made a start on the list as soon as she'd got home from school the day before. It was headed

100 REASONS WHY HAVING A DOG WOULD BE A REALLY, REALLY, REALLY GOOD IDEA.

Lizzie held up two thumbs – the sign for 'good'.

Ted grinned as he lifted Thumper out of the hutch and put him on the grass. The rabbit kicked up his back legs and went hopping off. Lizzie picked up Wriggles and put him on the grass too. Wriggles immediately went racing over to his friend Thumper.

Lizzie and Ted watched as the rabbits nibbled at the grass, while Ruby the cat

scowled at them from on top of the fence.

'What number are you up to on the dog list?' Ted signed.

Lizzie held up all her fingers and thumbs.

'Ten.'

Ted lived with his gran and they had five pets: as well as Thumper, Wriggles and Ruby, they also had two rats. Lizzie only wanted one dog. **Not much to ask!**

That's why she was making the list. She'd decorated it with stickers of dogs and lots of glitter, and written each of the reasons in a different coloured pen.

1. Dogs make you HAPPY.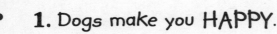

Lizzie was sure her mum and dad would want that!

2. Dogs are SMART.

Victor the hearing dog, who lived next door to Ted, was very smart indeed – and friendly too. His owner, Mrs Rose, said Victor knew over fifty different signs and commands.

As Lizzie refilled the rabbits' water bottle she thought that maybe if she filmed Victor on her phone, the footage would provide even *more* evidence to convince her parents to let her have a dog.

Mrs Rose and Victor were out shopping, just as they always were on Saturday mornings, so she couldn't film him yet. But on Saturday afternoons, Lizzie usually took Victor for a walk.

He was a very important example to add to her list, because Lizzie, her mum and her dad were all deaf. So why wouldn't her parents let her have an extremely helpful hearing dog like Victor? It was so unfair! They'd said maybe when she was older they'd think about it. Lizzie had been eight for ages now – *surely* that was old enough! In the meantime she'd just have to keep working on her parents. It was a mystery to her why she had to wait **SOOOOOOOO** long. Lizzie hoped the list would help solve her ***no-dog-yet*** problem.

3. Dogs are FUNNY.

4. Dogs are CUDDLY.

5. Dogs are FRIENDLY.

6. Dogs ALERT you to BURGLARS.

Number 6 was very important. Sometimes she'd lie awake at night worrying that a burglar might be trying to break into their house and none of them would be able to hear it. If they had a dog it could bark and come running into their rooms to let them know.

On the other hand, Lizzie was sure any burglar that met her dad would take one look at him and go racing straight back out of the front door! Her dad was six foot three and had fists as big as watermelons – or that's what he told his friends, anyway. Lizzie thought his fists could only really be the size of

baby watermelons, but she didn't say so to her dad because she knew he liked telling everyone about his watermelon fists.

7. You WALK MORE if you have a dog.

Mum and Dad were always saying they should get more exercise. Especially now they both worked from home as prop makers and designers.

8. You'll make NEW FRIENDS – hearing and deaf friends.

Lizzie had a lot of deaf friends, but not so many hearing ones – apart from Ted, of course. She looked at him and smiled as he spread fresh hay over the bottom of the rabbits' hutch. Ted was her best friend and he liked making lists almost as much as she did, when he wasn't building things. Ted had made the rabbits' hutch from spare wood and wire a while ago.

He'd once made a list of five reasons why rats were better than rabbits. And another list of five reasons why rabbits were better than rats. Ted's rats were called Gobbler and Jaws, and they loved eating raspberries, just as much as Thumper and Wriggles did. Ted couldn't decide whether he liked his rats or his rabbits best. Lizzie thought rats and rabbits were too different to compare.

And he wanted a dog too, but his gran said he couldn't have one because they had so many pets already.

9. Dogs can eat up scrap food so there's NO WASTE.

Lizzie wasn't really sure about this one. Her mum was very aware of climate change and made certain they did everything they could not to waste food. But some foods were bad for dogs. Like artificial sweeteners and chocolate. She'd have to draw up a list of things dogs could and couldn't eat for when she finally got one of her own. She didn't want to make her dog ill by mistake.

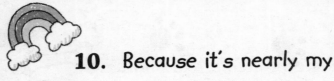

10. Because it's nearly my birthday (in a few months) and I want a dog more than ANYTHING in the whole world, and I will never ask for another present ever again if I could just have this one.

Please

please

please

please

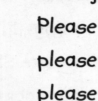

PLEASE.

Last year her favourite birthday present had been a hearing-aid headband, and charms with cute little dogs on them. But

12

this year she wanted a real dog!

'Do you want to stay for lunch, Lizzie?'
Ted's gran called from the back door. She
then made the sign for 'food' and
'eating' to Lizzie.

Lizzie shook her head. 'Better go
home,' she signed to Ted.

'See you later,' Ted signed back.

Lizzie headed out through the side gate
and across the road.

★

Upstairs in her room, Lizzie added more
glitter to the list and drew a picture of a
dog's smiling face at the end of what she
had written so far. It was time to show
her parents.

Bits of glitter fell off the list as Lizzie

went downstairs with it. She thought the sparkly effect made the stairs look much prettier.

Mum and Dad were in the kitchen drinking coffee and eating home-made gingerbread biscuits that had just come out of the oven.

'OK?' Mum signed to Lizzie with a smile. Her mum was much smaller than her dad and she had bright ruby-red hair. Sometimes she changed the colour to green or blue or purple or a mixture of them all. Sometimes she changed it to match her hearing-aid charms, which she called **bling**. It just depended on how she was feeling. Dad's hair was always light brown and so was his bushy beard. He had twinkly brown eyes and his face crinkled at the corners when he laughed, which he was always doing. He wasn't wearing his hearing aids but he was wearing his favourite earring. It was shaped like a pirate skull-and-crossbones flag.

Lizzie showed her parents the list.

Her dad rolled his eyes. 'Only ten?' he signed.

Lizzie shook her head as she helped herself to one of the freshly made biscuits. 'I can easily think of a hundred!'

They used sign language all the time in their house. It was just the same as speaking, but using your hands.

Dad signed back, 'One hundred and one — and then we'll see.'

Lizzie smiled as she crunched on her biscuit. She loved a challenge.

CHAPTER

Two streets away, a small black-and-white Dalmatian puppy trembled with fear as the ground raced beneath her . . .

★

Eight weeks ago, when she'd been born in Mrs Samuels' house, her eyes and ears had been closed. For two weeks she hadn't been able to see or hear her nine brothers and sisters because they all had their eyes and ears closed too. But she could feel them and she could sense her mother's soft, furry body close by.

None of the puppies had been able to walk for the first few weeks and had to paddle-crawl across the floor making little mewling sounds to their mother, who was never far away.

At two weeks old, the puppies' eyes and ears had finally opened. Their little black noses wrinkled as they sniffed the air around them.

'We need to see how much your puppies weigh, Molly,' Mrs Samuels told the mother dog.

Molly watched as Mrs Samuels carefully weighed each of the puppies every day to make sure none of

them were falling behind. The smiling
lady put a different coloured ribbon round
the neck of each puppy to identify them
more easily.

'A blue one for you . . . and a red . . . a
pink . . . a purple . . . a white . . . a yellow
. . . a black . . . an orange . . . a silver and
last of all a green for Little Girl Green,'
Mrs Samuels said.

Little Girl Green loved playing with her brothers and sisters. Sometimes they would play chase, running after each other on their short puppy legs. Sometimes, when the others were asleep and she'd had no one to play with, Little Girl Green tried chasing her own tail until she toppled over. However fast she ran, it was always just out of reach!

When Mrs Samuels saw her running in circles after her own tail she laughed and laughed. 'Well, look at you, Little Green, inventing a game all by yourself!'

Not long after that, Mrs Samuels put a puppy playpen out in the garden, and the puppies experienced fresh air for the first time and sniffed at the hundreds of

different smells that now swirled
around them.

Little Green looked up into the
sky as a butterfly danced above her.
She watched entranced until one of
her brothers, who had a black patch
of fur over one eye and an orange
ribbon round his neck, bit down on
her tail and she whizzed around to
chase and then pounce on top of him
instead. **Time to play!**

Soon, the Dalmatian puppies started to have visitors every day; there were lots of children and grown-ups. Gradually, one and then another and another of her brothers and sisters went to new homes. Little Green missed not having them to play with.

'You'll have a new home soon,' Mrs Samuels told her.

★

As the days turned warmer, Little Green's favourite place to play was the garden. There were so many interesting smells to sniff at and spots to explore. Her mother and Mrs Samuels were always there to watch over her.

One day, Mrs Samuels was tending her

plants and Little Green was trying to help by digging too.

'Well, look at the state of you,' Mrs Samuels laughed. Little Green was covered with mud. 'Time for a cup of tea and a biscuit, I think. I'll see if I can find something tasty for you two as well.'

Mrs Samuels went into the house and shut the back door. Molly closed her eyes and drifted off to sleep in the sunspot on the patio.

A butterfly fluttered past Little Green and she chased it across the small garden. She watched as the butterfly flew over the low back fence and away. Little Green sat down and gave a whine. Maybe one day the butterfly might play with her, but not today! She was still looking in the direction of the butterfly when two hands suddenly appeared over the fence and scooped her up. The puppy let out a yelp of fear! Her little legs scrabbled desperately in the air as the garden disappeared from view. She wriggled but couldn't get free.

Molly's eyes snapped open and she jumped up, barking and growling as she ran over to help her daughter.

The noise brought Mrs Samuels
hurrying from the kitchen, but it was too
late. **LITTLE GREEN
WAS GONE!**

CHAPTER 3

While Lizzie was waiting to get her own dog, *one day*, she was practising by helping to look after other people's pets. Her noticeboard was covered with drawings and notes about each of them so she wouldn't forget what they liked to do, eat and play with.

RUBY

TED'S GRAN'S ELDERLY TABBY CAT

Sometimes she likes cuddles, sometimes not. Sometimes she likes playing with her string toy, sometimes not. Likes sitting on iPads. (Do not take Dad's with you again.) Not to be given too many treats.

IGGY

GRAN AND GRANDAD'S IGUANA

Seven years old. If she's lost, check warm spots. Likes to eat strawberries and is VERY good at escaping.

BOO
GRAN AND GRANDAD'S PARROT
Very, very old. His favourite food is walnuts (not too many).

Iggy and Boo were the best of friends, so much so that Iggy didn't even mind when Boo helped himself to her food.

THUMPER and WRIGGLES
TED'S RABBITS
Like raspberries (not too many) and the garden (though they sometimes try to escape)!

GOBBLER and JAWS

TED'S RATS

Like raspberries and their toys.
Very good at hiding.

VICTOR

MRS ROSE'S YELLOW
LABRADOR HEARING DOG

Six years old. Loves water and
getting muddy (when he's allowed
to – Mrs Rose says a muddy
dog in the supermarket is NOT
popular)! Likes walks (lots) and
dog treats but he's not allowed
too many.

Lizzie loved Victor. He was the best-behaved and cleverest dog she'd ever met. As well as her notes about him, she had a photograph of Victor that she'd stuck on the wall behind her bed, along with lots of other pictures of different dogs.

Just then, Lizzie's phone flashed. She had a text message from Mrs Rose.

Victor's ready for his walk when you are.

Lizzie ran down the stairs, waved goodbye to her parents, and checked both ways before crossing the road to Victor's house.

'If I had a pet like Victor,' Lizzie signed

to Mrs Rose when she got there, 'I could teach it to be a hearing dog.'

Mrs Rose said she thought that would be an excellent idea. Lizzie could mostly lip-read her because she spoke very clearly. Mrs Rose hadn't lost her hearing until she was a grown-up, but now she could hardly hear at all. Mrs Rose said one of the many good things about having Victor was that everyone realized she was deaf because of his *Hearing Dog* jacket.

'Otherwise people might think I was just ignoring them!'

Lizzie gave Victor a stroke and he wagged his tail.

'If you get a dog, I'll help you train it to be a hearing dog, if you like,' Mrs Rose said.

Lizzie put her thumbs up and nodded – she'd like that very much.

Victor padded over to the front door and looked back at Lizzie. It was time to go for a walk.

Lizzie clipped the Labrador's lead to his collar and they set off down the street in the direction of the wildflower meadow, where there'd once been a castle a long, long time ago. All that was left now was a bit of wall and a plaque, but the meadow was bursting with wildflowers and different grasses, as well as lots of insects, birds and probably some other animals too. Lizzie hoped so and she kept an eye out for them, although she hadn't seen any other animals yet.

Lizzie and Victor were almost at the meadow when she spotted a grubby white van parked in the lay-by close to the castle ruins.

What was it doing there?

Lizzie wondered. Hardly anyone came to look at the ruins because there wasn't really very much left to see.

Victor suddenly stopped dead and stared to the right. Lizzie could feel him tense up. Her gaze followed the direction of Victor's – and just at that moment, a man came running out of the alleyway that ran along behind the houses.

He was carrying A PUPPY under his arm!

Victor opened his mouth and barked. Lizzie had never seen him do that before. She could only just hear him through her hearing aids, but she could see his mouth, and his face looked all snarly. Victor clearly didn't like the look of the man and neither did Lizzie. Something was wrong.

Why was he running with a puppy under his arm? It wasn't safe. What if he fell? The puppy could be injured!

But the man didn't seem to care about that. He pulled the van door open, threw the puppy inside, and then jumped into the driver's seat.

Lizzie was sure something wasn't right, but she didn't know what to do. Then she had a flash of inspiration – she could take a photo of the van's number plate! Lizzie pulled her phone from her pocket and pressed the camera button . . . but it was too late. The van was already speeding off into the distance and all she'd managed to get was a blurry picture of the back of it.

Lizzie looked at Victor, sighed, and bit

her bottom lip. The number plate was impossible to read. Then, realizing she could at least remember the first part of it – RV02 – Lizzie quickly typed it into her phone before it slipped her mind. If only she'd got it all! Why was the man running out of the alleyway carrying a puppy?

Something was definitely NOT RIGHT.

CHAPTER  4

The loud noise as the engine rattled and roared harshly into life hurt Little Green's sensitive ears. She wanted to be back with her mum, not with this man who had snatched her from the garden. She didn't like him at all!

As the van raced off down the street, Little Green felt a swirly feeling in her tummy and the next moment she was sick on the floor.

'BAD PUPPY!' the man snarled.

Then, all of a sudden,
the van screeched to a
brake-squealing halt
outside the garage of a
run-down house.

Little Green yelped
when the man grabbed her
again. Then he unlocked
the garage roller-door
and yanked it open.

Inside the concrete-
floored, windowless room,
Little Green saw many
pairs of eyes blinking at
her from cages crammed
together and stacked one
on top of the other.

Her nose sniffed as it detected a new smell, one she hadn't known before. It was the smell of fear coming from the dogs trapped inside the garage.

The man opened the door of a small empty cage, put Little Green inside and bolted it shut. The puppy didn't want to be imprisoned in a cage and yapped to be let out. Then the other dogs started whining and barking too.

'SHUT UP!'

the man shouted and with that he pulled the garage roller-door back down and locked it, plunging the dogs into darkness.

Fortunately, Little Green's eyes were

five times better at seeing in the dark than a human's, so she could still make out the other dogs all around her.

The puppy whimpered. She wanted to be back home with her mum and Mrs Samuels, playing in her garden. Not here. She bit as hard as she could at the cage bars.

A very old Cavalier King Charles spaniel in the next cage was biting at the bars of her own prison. Other dogs in the garage were doing the same. All of them were determined to get out, but the metal was too strong.

At last, Little Green headed to the side of her cage that was closest to the spaniel and they sniffed noses through the bars.

When the spaniel lay down to rest Little Green lay down too. She pushed a paw out to the spaniel and the spaniel pushed a paw out to her. Their paw pads touched and they were as close together as they could be, separated only by the cages' metal bars.

CHAPTER 5

When Lizzie and Victor got back, she told Mrs Rose what she'd seen.

'Victor barked. I could see he didn't like the man,' Lizzie signed.

Mrs Rose shook her head. That wasn't like Victor at all. Mrs Rose wasn't very confident about using sign language yet, although she was taking a class and could understand a lot. She made the sign for 'dangerous' and Lizzie nodded.

★

Back home, Lizzie's mum and dad shook their heads too when they'd understood what had happened.

Lizzie wished she'd remembered more of the van's number plate.

'Maybe it's nothing,' her mum signed, putting an arm round her worried daughter and giving a squeeze. 'Maybe the puppy was sick and the man was running to the vet's to get help.'

Lizzie looked at her dad and he agreed.

'That *could* be it,' Lizzie frowned. 'The puppy could have

been very poorly or swallowed something bad. Perhaps the man had to run if the puppy was going to survive. He was trying to save it.' Lizzie tried to smile, but she couldn't because the explanation just didn't feel quite right. She was determined to investigate further, although she wasn't exactly sure how.

She showed her mum and dad the partial number plate she'd typed into her phone. They were looking at it just as a text message came through from Ted.

Animal Rescue Centre open afternoon today at 3!?!

Lizzie's eyes widened. Maybe if her mum and dad met some of the dogs at the rescue centre looking for a home, they'd finally let her get one of her own.

'Open afternoon?' Mum signed.

Lizzie's eyes shone and she nodded. She was desperate to go to the open afternoon, despite being really worried about the puppy.

'Let's all go,' signed her dad.

Lizzie nodded and texted Ted.

★

Soon afterwards, she was running up the path to Ted's house to knock for him while her mum and dad were getting into the car.

Ted opened the front door, looking

46

worried, and beckoned her inside.

'OK?' Lizzie signed to him.

Ted shook his head. 'Gobbler's lost,' he said as Lizzie lip-read his words.

He ran up the stairs to his room with Lizzie right behind.

It wouldn't have mattered too much if one of Ted's rats had escaped somewhere inside the house, but for the fact that Ruby the cat lived under the same roof.

'Gobbler was in there,' Ted said, pointing to the plastic drainpipe he'd fixed from the rats' cage along his bedroom wall.

Lizzie stood on the bed so she could peek inside the opening at the top of the pipe. Gobbler didn't seem to be anywhere

But then she noticed that the curtain at Ted's window was touching the pipe. Gobbler must have squeezed his way out and scrambled up there.

'Stepladder,' she signed.

Ted ran to fetch it and Lizzie climbed to the top of the ladder to get a better look.

Just as she had expected, Gobbler was at the very top of the curtains. He'd got stuck between the folds, but didn't seem to be injured at all. In fact, he was busily cleaning his whiskers.

Lizzie stretched out her hand and Gobbler crept on to it.

'Thanks,' Ted signed, looking very relieved. 'Good detective work, Lizzie.'

He put Gobbler back
in the cage with Jaws,
who immediately ran
over to sniff at his friend
and start grooming him.

It was then that Ted
became aware of a car
horn honking over and over
outside. **'Uh-oh,'** he
said to Lizzie, miming her
dad looking angry and
pressing the horn. Lizzie
grinned – Dad never
seemed to appreciate
that the noise was a lot

louder for hearing people. They ran down the stairs and out of the house before the neighbours started complaining!

★

There were already lots of people at the open afternoon and a long queue of cars waiting to get into the field car park when they arrived. Lizzie wondered if the white van would be there. Maybe the man was taking the puppy to the rescue centre. Maybe she didn't need to be worried. But she was, and she couldn't see the van anywhere.

What she *could* see was her dad's hand hovering over the horn, ready to tell

everyone to hurry up. But her mum touched him on the arm, pointed at the horn and shook her head. Lizzie could tell by the way her dad grinned that Mum had only just been in time.

Once the car was parked, they followed the crowds heading towards the colourful flags decorating the fences of the animal rescue centre.

CHAPTER 6

They decided to have a look around the amusement stalls first. Ted had a go at the hoopla and nearly won a tube of Smarties.

Lizzie caught a yellow plastic duck with a mini fishing rod and had her pick of the prizes laid out on the table.

Ted pointed to a small wooden caterpillar toy. 'For Gobbler and Jaws,' he said as Lizzie lip-read him. She nodded, sure that Ted's rats would love it.

'Thanks,' Ted grinned as she gave it to him.

Next, they headed over to the food stall. Mum and Dad had lemon drizzle cake, but Lizzie and Ted decided on a box of multicoloured popcorn.

At the sanctuary, there were two big pigs and some cows and sheep, as well as rabbits, guinea pigs, chickens and baby goats that made cute little bleating sounds and jumped about. Lizzie wanted to give them some of her popcorn, but there were signs everywhere saying,

PLEASE DON'T FEED THE ANIMALS.

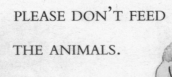

After that, they came to the cats, who
were all in one big enclosure together,
surrounded by lots of little flowerpots of
grass.

'Why?' Dad signed, his face
frowning.

Ted asked a member
of staff, who wore a name tag
that said MARY.

'It's cat grass and catnip,'
Mary told him. 'The cats like it
and it helps to soothe them.'

Lizzie thought maybe Ted's cat, Ruby, would like some too.

Then they moved on to the dogs, who were wagging their tails and barking from inside glass-fronted kennels. A Jack Russell cross licked at the glass when Lizzie put her palm on it. She glanced at his water bowl, worrying that the dog might be thirsty. She was pleased to see the water bowl was full. Not thirsty, just saying hello.

There were so many animals at the rescue centre and all of them were hoping for a good home. Lizzie felt sorry for the poor creatures, suddenly confronted by all these people looking and pointing at them. She would hate to be in a cage being stared at by crowds of nosy onlookers.

'I'd like to take all the animals home,' Ted said as Lizzie lip-read him. She smiled and nodded, pointing to herself and holding her thumbs up. She felt just the same.

There was a talk on first aid for animals, but there wasn't a sign-language interpreter, so Lizzie picked up a leaflet instead. She'd collected lots of different information sheets throughout the day. In fact, when Mary, the staff member they'd spoken to in the cat section, saw all the brochures Lizzie was holding, she gave her a tote bag bearing the animal rescue centre's logo to carry them in.

'Thank you,' Lizzie signed to her, and Mary smiled.

One of the leaflets was about **dog thieves** and **puppy farming**.

Lizzie thought of the little Dalmatian she'd seen. Was that man running with the puppy under his arm a dog thief? Was the poor little thing being stolen? She wished, not for the first time, that she'd remembered all of the van's number plate. Maybe then she could have gone to the police. Or at least let the staff at the animal rescue centre know. They might have been able to help.

She went back to join Mum, Dad and Ted.

Lizzie showed them the leaflet about

dog thieves and puppy farms.

'People like that should go to prison,' signed her dad, and Lizzie and Ted agreed.

Their next stop was at a kennel containing a Rottweiler. The dog sat down and put his paw out to Lizzie's dad, who grinned, crouched and extended his hand to the animal.

'Friendly dog,' he signed to Lizzie as

he looked up at her from his crouching
position. But then his brow creased as
he lip-read what some hearing people
standing behind them were saying.

Ted had overheard the remarks
as well and his face turned red with
embarrassment.

'What?' Lizzie signed to Ted as the
speakers moved on and her dad stood up.

'They asked if a deaf person would be
able to look after a dog. How would a
deaf person know
if the dog was
barking or
whimpering?'
her friend replied
as Lizzie lip-read.

'Of course we would!' Lizzie's dad signed back.

Ted nodded; he already knew that.

Lizzie could see her dad was angry. He hated it when anyone assumed he couldn't do something just because he was deaf. Deaf people could do everything a hearing person could do – apart from hear! Dad started to follow the group that had been so rude, but Lizzie's mum stopped him.

'Time to go home, then,' Dad signed. They all agreed.

★

When Lizzie went to sleep that night she dreamed of the little Dalmatian stuffed under the man's arm. The grubby white

60

van kept rushing past her, but she could never catch it.

When Lizzie woke up the next day, she was more determined than ever to find the van and the puppy, and solve the mystery.

CHAPTER 7

Little Green shivered with cold and fear inside the cage. She'd never slept away from her mother before and she missed her comforting presence. There was no telling whether it was day or night inside the dark garage, but the other imprisoned dogs around her had been barking and whining for a long time when the door was finally opened and a burst of light came in.

'SHUT UP!' shouted the same

man who'd stolen her. The sound of his angry voice terrified Little Green.

'**YOU!**' the man growled as he unbolted her cage.

The puppy cowered, but there was nowhere to hide as he reached inside.

The old Cavalier King Charles spaniel in the next cage whined as Little Green was lifted out, but it didn't make any difference. The puppy looked back at the spaniel and whimpered as the man took her away and closed the garage.

The back doors of the van were already open and Little Green could see lots of other caged dogs inside the vehicle.

'In you go,' the man said, opening a cage that already contained four other puppies – two bigger and two smaller ones. He pushed Little Green inside and bolted the door.

★

Lizzie left a note for her mum and dad when she let herself out of the house early in the morning. She took a pair of washing-up gloves with her and a bag for any clues she found.

The last place she'd seen the puppy was the lay-by near the castle ruins. So she set off in that direction, hoping some evidence might have been left behind.

It was so early that no one else was about when she arrived.

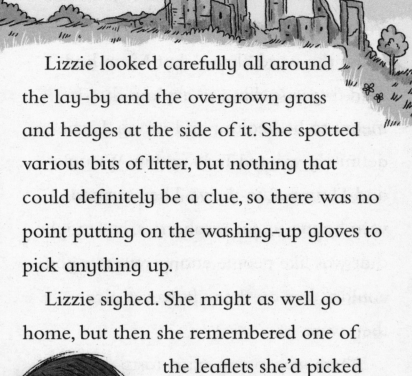

Lizzie looked carefully all around
the lay-by and the overgrown grass
and hedges at the side of it. She spotted
various bits of litter, but nothing that
could definitely be a clue, so there was no
point putting on the washing-up gloves to
pick anything up.

Lizzie sighed. She might as well go
home, but then she remembered one of
the leaflets she'd picked
up at the animal rescue
centre. It was about
rabbits needing

to have lots of fresh grass if they were
to thrive and be happy. Lizzie didn't
know the word 'thrive', but Mum had
used finger-spelling to explain that it
meant to be healthy and strong. Lizzie
definitely wanted Ted's rabbits, Wriggles
and Thumper, to thrive. They seemed
very happy to eat raspberries, but maybe
that was like people eating sweets – you
couldn't live on them, however nice
they were.

There was lots of extra-tasty-looking,
very long meadow grass with wildflowers
growing in it here by the castle ruins and
Lizzie was sure Thumper and Wriggles
would love to eat it. She started picking
some and putting it in her clue bag.

She'd collected quite
a lot when in the
distance she saw a van
heading down the street
and her heart started
to race.

'RV02 . . .' she read on the number plate
once the van was close enough. 'NYO.'
Now she was certain it *was* the right one!

Lizzie lay down in the long grass and
wildflowers so she wouldn't be seen and
took out her phone. The van pulled into
a lay-by and the same man she'd seen
yesterday got out. She watched as he
checked all around for passers-by before
opening the back doors. Luckily, he hadn't
spotted her.

Lizzie risked a peek and was horrified to see a number of caged dogs inside. **What are they DOING in there?** she wondered. If the man was a dog warden or worked for an animal rescue society, then he'd have a van that had an official name painted on the side. This one didn't have any lettering. So what was he doing and why did he have all those poor animals?

Lizzie was sure he must be a dog thief. She quickly took a photo of the van's full number plate just as a second vehicle drew up in the lay-by. Safely hidden in the long grass, Lizzie used her phone to video the man pulling a dog from a cage by the scruff of its neck and giving

it to the driver of the car in exchange
for some money. She ducked her head
as they looked all around to make sure
they hadn't been seen. Then the car
drove off with the dog inside it, but
Lizzie didn't dare move while the van
was still there.

Minutes later, a red hatchback pulled
up and this time it was not just one dog
that was exchanged, but three.

Lizzie knew she had to do something.

CHAPTER 8

The cage containing the five puppies was very cramped. Little Green couldn't move at all unless she crawled over some of the other puppies.

She cowered fearfully into the corner when the back door of the van was opened and a hand reached inside. The other puppies tried to get away too. None of them wanted to be taken, but there wasn't much space in the small cage to hide.

'GOT YOU!'

Little Green squealed and tried to get away as the man grabbed her tail. He pulled her towards him and then gripped tightly as he took her from the cage.

'No point resisting,' he said as she wriggled and squirmed to get away.

In response, Little Green's sharp puppy teeth bit his hand as hard as she could and he yelled out in pain.

'YOU . . .!'

He dropped her on to the ground and before he could catch her, Little Green was off, running across the lay-by to the

wildflower meadow beyond. Her heart was racing and her legs were stumbling and stiff from being kept in the cage, but she was determined. Determined she was not going to be caught. Determined she was not going back. Determined to get away.

Lizzie watched as another car drove into the lay-by. It had a light on the roof and letters along the side.

Little Green didn't stop. She ran into the long grass and wildflowers and when she saw Lizzie, she raced into her arms. The puppy didn't know why, but she

knew she could trust this girl in the grass.
Little Green was trembling with fear and
excited all at the same time –

she had
ESCAPED!

CHAPTER 9

The puppy kept very close to Lizzie as they went into the kitchen. She peeped out at the new people from behind the girl's legs, but wasn't brave enough to go over to them.

She let the lady with red hair stroke her, but when the big man stretched out his hand she skittered away, frightened. He patted his leg and beckoned, but still she didn't go to him, not even when he pulled a sad face and made funny little **cooing** sounds.

'Frightened,' Lizzie signed, and her
mum and dad nodded.

She told her mum and dad what had
happened. 'A police car drove into the lay-
by, but the officers didn't question or arrest
the bad man. They just drove off again a
few minutes later.'

As Lizzie was relating her story, the
puppy started sniffing the air. Mum and
Dad had been eating toast.

Lizzie gave the puppy a bit of leftover
toast and she crunched it up
with her sharp white
teeth.

'Thirsty?' signed
Lizzie's dad, filling a
small bowl with water.

Lizzie put the water in front of the
puppy and her little tongue lapped
eagerly.

Lizzie's mum looked in the fridge
for something tasty and healthy for the
puppy to eat.

The puppy drank and drank, but the

next moment lots of the water came out of her mouth and landed on the kitchen floor. The puppy shrank in fear, as she looked down at the cloudy water with toast crumbs floating in it on the floor and then back at the three people.

Lizzie quickly got a paper towel to mop the floor and gave the puppy a reassuring stroke as she made soothing noises to her.

Lizzie's mum and dad thought it would be best if they got the puppy checked at the vet's. 'Could be ill,' her dad signed. 'Don't know how it ended up in the van or where it was before.'

Mum used SignLive to contact the surgery that Lizzie had visited with Mrs Rose a few months ago, when Victor had

his yearly health check. She had the app
on her phone for making appointments,
or for any situation when she needed to
have her signs translated to a hearing
person. There were a few different apps
like that. Mum used the camera on her
phone to sign to an online interpreter,
who then spoke for her to the receptionist
at the vet's. Luckily, the surgery had some
availability and told Mum to bring the
puppy in straight away.

Technology made booking
appointments much easier these days!

★

Mum and Lizzie sat in the back of the car
with the puppy while Dad drove.

Everyone from the receptionist to the

nurse and even the vet herself made lots
of **Oohing** and **aaahing** noises
as soon as they saw the puppy. Lizzie
couldn't hear their voices, but she could
see their mouth shapes and smiling faces.

Little Green wagged her tail as they
made a big fuss of her and stroked her. She
thought the vet's was a very nice place,
but she was still so hungry.

Dad showed the staff a card saying
they were deaf and the vet nodded and
beckoned them into the treatment room.

Mum put a notebook and pen on the
table so if they couldn't lip-read what the
vet was saying she could write it down,
and they could also use it to ask their
own questions.

The vet listened to Little Green's heart
and checked her teeth, eyes, legs and paws.
She even took her temperature, which the
puppy didn't like very much.

'She seems healthy,' the vet concluded, 'and she's got a microchip number, so we should be able to find her real owner on one of the databases soon. Whoever she was stolen from will probably want her back – but that isn't always the case. If she was owned by a criminal, they certainly won't claim her.'

Then Lizzie showed the vet the photo of the white van's number plate and the vet made a note of it and said she'd report what had happened to the authorities. In the meantime, though, they could take the puppy home. Lizzie secretly hoped that the little Dalmatian's original owner wouldn't be found. Now she actually had a dog, Lizzie didn't want to lose her. But then she thought about how she'd feel if it had been her pet that was stolen. She'd be devastated and desperate to get it back.

'Just make sure you don't overtire her – twenty minutes' walking and then a rest,' the vet advised. 'Little and often is best for puppies of this age – especially when we don't know what trauma she's been through. Puppies who are kept in cages all the time don't have the chance for their muscles and bones to develop properly.'

Lizzie thought about the other poor dogs still stuck in the van. What about their muscles and bones? What would happen to them?

'Puppy food?' Mum wrote.

'Which is tastiest?' Dad added and the

vet picked a bag of puppy food for them with a smile.

'What are you going to call her?' the vet asked Lizzie as they were leaving. 'She'll need a name other than "Puppy", even if you only have her for a short while.'

Lizzie lip-read the question, had a think and then signed **'Lucky'**. She wrote it down so the vet could see, all the time hoping she was going to be lucky too and that the little dog wouldn't be taken away from her.

The vet smiled and nodded and Lucky wagged her tail as they headed out.

CHAPTER 10

When they got home, Lizzie put some of Lucky's new puppy food in a bowl for her and made the sign for 'food', while the little dog watched. As soon as Lizzie put the bowl down, Lucky's little head went straight in and the meal was quickly gone.

After she'd eaten, Lizzie took Lucky out into the garden. There were lots of butterflies dancing around the lavender bush and the puppy ran over to them. Lizzie followed her as Lucky explored

the garden. But it wasn't long before the
puppy fell fast asleep in the flower bed.
Lizzie and her mum and dad watched
over her as she slept.

'Sweet,' Lizzie's dad signed as the
puppy's chest rose and fell.

'Lucky she found us,' signed Lizzie.

'Good name for her,' signed Lizzie's mum.

Lizzie texted Ted to tell him she was looking after a puppy. What felt like two seconds later, the front-doorbell alert started flashing.

Lizzie smiled, but didn't want to leave Lucky, so Mum went to open the door instead.

Ted came running into the garden, then stopped dead, his mouth opening wide when he saw Lucky sleeping. Lizzie put her fingers to her lips. Ted put his fingers to his lips too and then sat next to Lizzie on the ground to admire the tiny dog. They watched as Lucky's legs started **twitching**, and then as she made little crying sounds that only Ted could hear.

When the puppy eventually opened
her eyes, three people who'd been kind
to her and one boy, with shiny eyes, were
watching.

Lucky gazed at Lizzie, stood up
unsteadily, wagged her tail and then
padded over and curled herself into the
girl's lap as her new friend stroked her.

'**Wow,**' Ted signed. '**WOW.**'

Lizzie's mum showed him the notebook they'd taken to the vet's, in which they'd written the whole story of Lucky's escape — or at least as much of it as they knew.

Ted shook his head in amazement. 'You're a good detective,' he told Lizzie, not for the first time.

Lizzie held up her thumbs and grinned as she lip-read. She liked being a detective.

Ted pretended to be Lizzie lying in the long grass, spying on the bad man and photographing him with her phone.

'Puppy thieves should go to prison,' Lizzie's dad signed again and Ted nodded.

Lizzie stroked Lucky's soft fur. She loved

her so much already and really hoped she
didn't have to give the Dalmatian back to
her original owner.

★

Once Lucky was fully awake it was time
for her next meal.

'She loves food!' Ted signed and Lizzie
laughed.

Lizzie was so happy that Lucky had
come to live with them, but she was
worried too. What if the thief with the
white van came looking for her? What
if he tried to steal her back? Lizzie
hoped the vet had given the van's
number plate to the police and that
they'd caught him.

Then she remembered the long grass

she'd picked for Thumper and Wriggles and gave it to Ted.

'Back soon,' Ted said, taking the bag with him.

Ten minutes later, the doorbell activated the flashing light on the kitchen wall, alerting Lizzie to his return. Lucky glanced at it and then back at Lizzie, who grinned and held her thumbs up. Lucky wagged her tail.

Ted came in with lots of things for Lucky in a big bag.

He pulled out Ruby's cat collar first. 'Ruby hates it and won't let Gran put it on her,' Ted said.

Lizzie put the collar round Lucky's neck. It was just the right size for a young

Dalmatian puppy.

Dad went online
to order a name
tag. 'Arrives
tomorrow,' he
signed.

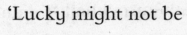

'Lucky might not be
here by then,' Lizzie signed back.

'Might,' Dad signed and crossed his
fingers.

Lizzie shook her head. The vet had said
that the puppy had been microchipped –
if Lucky's real owner was found, she'd
have to go back.

Lizzie swallowed hard . . .

what if Lucky's real owner was the man
with the white van? What if Lucky was

really his? But then why did he have all those other dogs in the van too?

It was still a mystery – a mystery that needed to be solved.

'And I thought Lucky might like some toys to play with,' Ted said, pulling out cat toys and rat toys and a small ball. 'I didn't bring the caterpillar toy because it's too rat-chewed,' he told Lizzie.

Lastly he pulled out a toy that looked a bit like an octopus, but only had four long legs that were

perfect for a puppy to hold on to.

Lizzie made the sign for **'WOW'**. Ted
had brought so many things.

'Mrs Rose gave me that last one. I told
her about the puppy and she said Victor
had been given two of these, so Lucky
could have this one. It's a tug toy and she
said it was virtually indestructible.'

'Thank you,' signed Lizzie, looking
at all the things he'd brought. She didn't
want Lucky to be parted from them,
not ever.

Lucky sniffed at her new toys before picking up the four-legged octopus.

'You loved your comfort blanket when you were little,' Mum signed as she got Lizzie's comfort blanket out of the drawer where she'd kept it as a keepsake. Lucky put down the octopus and sniffed at the blanket, her tail wagging. When Lizzie gave it to her she carried it around and then curled up on it.

'She likes it because it smells of you, Lizzie,' Ted said.

'I DON'T SMELL!' Lizzie signed.

Ted shook his head. 'I don't mean a bad smell – a nice smell. It reminds her of her friend,' he signed back.

Lucky tilted her head to one side and

then the other as she watched Lizzie, her parents and Ted moving their hands about as they spoke to each other in sign language.

Lizzie watched as the puppy looked up at her dad. His face was all screwed up. He opened his mouth and **wrinkled** his nose. Lucky suddenly went running across the room with her tail between her legs.

Dad frowned and Mum looked surprised, but Ted started laughing and made the signs for 'sneeze' and 'loud'.

Lizzie held her arms out to Lucky and the puppy came back, wagging her tail for a cuddle. Lizzie wasn't frightened by the strange sound coming from the big man's nose, so Lucky decided that she wouldn't be frightened either.

Lizzie's dad came over and picked the
puppy up, and gave her a stroke. For a
moment she struggled to get down, but
then she looked up at him and gave his
face fur a cautious puppy lick.

CHAPTER 11

The message alert light on Mum's phone flashed a few minutes later and she looked at it and then at Lizzie.

'What?' Lizzie signed to her, and Mum held out her phone so she could read the message. It was from the vet.

> The puppy's owner has been
> contacted and would like to come
> and collect it with someone from
> the animal rescue centre. Will you
> be in this afternoon?

Lizzie shook her
head as tears ran
down her face. She
didn't want Lucky
to be taken away.
Lizzie knelt down and
hugged the puppy to her.
If they were only going
to have Lucky with them for a little while,
then they'd better make sure the time was
full of fun.

She picked up the ball Ted had brought,
and Lucky danced after her and Ted as
they went out into the garden to play.

At first the puppy wasn't sure what
she was supposed to do when Lizzie
threw the ball, so she just looked up

at Lizzie and wagged her tail.

Lizzie laughed and pointed to the ball. Lucky looked over to where she was pointing, and then up at Lizzie again, wagging her tail.

Ted went to fetch the ball instead. The next time Lizzie threw the ball, Ted went running after it, making lots of excited noises.

Lucky watched him with her head tilted to one side. **'YES!'** Ted shouted, when he reached the ball, picking it up and running back with it.

All the time they played, Lizzie was secretly dreading the arrival of Lucky's owner. But she didn't want Lucky to feel sad, so she did her absolute best to keep smiling.

She still wondered how Lucky's owner could have lost her and how the puppy ended up in the van. It was a mystery.

★

An hour later, the bell rang and Lucky ran to the front door and then back to Lizzie.

Lizzie's dad opened the door to find Mary from the animal rescue centre standing there, wearing her *Animal Rescuer* uniform. With her was a sign-language interpreter called Jamie and an anxious lady called Mrs Samuels, with a dog that looked a lot like an adult version of Lucky.

Lizzie took a deep, steadying breath. Lucky's tail started wagging and wagging. She ran over to the older dog as Lizzie's dad beckoned everyone inside.

'That's Molly, her mother,' Mrs Samuels said as Jamie signed.

Lucky was overjoyed to see her mum and Molly made soft, happy, growly sounds deep in her throat. Jamie described the sounds in sign language and Ted grinned.

'Lucky's really pleased to see her mum,' Ted said.

'Lucky?' Mrs Samuels said.

'That's what Lizzie called her — she's the one who rescued Lucky. The puppy was trapped in a van and was just about to be handed over to someone in a car, but she escaped and ran to Lizzie instead. Lizzie's a really good detective. She wrote down the car's number plate and videoed the stolen dogs,' Ted explained, and Mrs Samuels nodded.

Lizzie felt sad and happy all at the same time.

'I like the name Lucky,' Mrs Samuels said and Jamie translated. 'I used to call her Little Girl Green or Little Green for short. I knew once she went to her forever home she'd be given a new name.'

Mrs Samuels watched as Lucky kept running over to Lizzie, then back to Molly and back to Lizzie again. 'I can see she means a lot to you already . . . and you to her,' she added with a smile.

'Tea?' Lizzie's mum signed and she put the kettle on.

But Lizzie didn't want a drink. Her throat felt like it had a lump in it and her eyes felt gritty with unshed tears. She kissed the top of Lucky's furry little head, determined not to cry.

She needed to be strong for Lucky.

CHAPTER 12

'Lucky was playing in the back garden when someone stole her,' Mrs Samuels said. 'She couldn't have escaped by herself. I'd only been indoors for a few minutes when I heard Molly barking over by the back fence and when I came out I immediately realized that Lucky had gone.'

'Terrible,' signed Lizzie's dad, when the interpreter had translated what she'd said. Everyone nodded sadly.

Lizzie and Ted watched Lucky and Molly playing with the four-legged octopus tug toy. They were pulling it back and forth gently between them.

Mum handed round tea and juice, and Dad got out the biscuits.

'Where do you live?' Lizzie's dad signed to Mrs Samuels. Jamie translated.

'Oh, not far away,' Mrs Samuels said. 'My house backs on to the alleyway near the castle ruins . . .'

'That's where I first saw Lucky!' Lizzie signed excitedly, although she hadn't known the puppy was Lucky at the time. But it must have been. 'I couldn't get the van's whole number plate then, but I remembered part of it.'

'Thank goodness you were there to see,' Mrs Samuels said.

'Hopefully the villain will be caught soon,' Mary from the rescue centre added. 'When I see how happy Lucky is now, I can't help thinking about all the awful things that might have happened to her if you hadn't been there. She could have ended up in one of those terrible puppy farms where the poor dogs are expected to have litter after litter until they're too old and then –'

Lizzie's mum shook her head and Jamie stopped signing. Mary changed the subject as Lucky brought the ball over to Lizzie and Ted.

Lizzie rolled it along the floor, then Lucky pushed it back with her nose.

Mrs Samuels chuckled. 'Much easier than fetch! It looks like you and Lucky were meant to be together.'

Lizzie nodded because that was exactly what she thought too.

Lucky padded over and rested her chin on Lizzie's leg, and Lizzie gave her a stroke.

'Looking after a puppy can be very hard work,' Mrs Samuels said, via Jamie. 'Someone needs to be with them. They shouldn't just be left alone at home all day. Puppies get lonely.'

'And can get into trouble and cause a lot of damage,' Mary added.

'We work from home,' Lizzie's mum signed.

'Do you indeed?' Mrs Samuels said, and she gave a little smile. 'And would you, perhaps, be interested in looking after a puppy?'

'YES!' Lizzie blurted out, lip-reading her.

Ted looked like he couldn't believe his ears.

Mum and Dad nodded and held up their thumbs. 'We love Lucky,' signed Dad.

'Well, so long as you promise to come and visit so Lucky can see her mum, and agree to meet up in the park every now and again for picnics and such, I don't see why Lucky . . .'

'. . . Couldn't stay here?' signed Lizzie, hardly able to believe it. A tear of happiness rolled down her face and she quickly pushed it away before jumping up to throw her arms round Mrs Samuels. **'Thank you!'**

'YES!' Ted exclaimed. He held his thumbs up and grinned and grinned.

'I can see Lucky's happy here and that's all I want for any of my dogs,' Mrs Samuels added.

And Lucky certainly was!

'Any clues about the dog thief? Or sightings of the van?' Mum asked Mary, with Jamie interpreting.

Mary sighed and shook her head. 'Not yet, but we're on the lookout,' she said.

Lizzie stroked Lucky. She was going to be on the lookout for that van too. There'd been more dogs inside it, not just Lucky, and they needed rescuing too. Lizzie was determined to get to the bottom of the missing puppies mystery once and for all.

CHAPTER 13

By the next morning Lucky had given
Lizzie three more reasons to add to her list.

11. Having a puppy sleeping
next to you is the best!

12. Playing in the middle of the
night is fun. (Lucky thinks
this is a particularly
good idea.)

13. Waking up and seeing a
cute furry face next to
you is great.

Lucky cuddled up next to Lizzie as she
wrote with different coloured pens on a
big piece of glittery paper. But as soon
as Lizzie made the sign for 'food', Lucky
raced to the bedroom door.

She loved food!

'That puppy eats fast!' signed Dad as
Lucky crunched on her dog biscuits.

'Hungry,' signed Lizzie as she crunched
on her own cereal.

After breakfast it was time for Lizzie to
go to school. Lucky thought she was going

too and tried to follow, but Lizzie gave the
puppy a big stroke, then went out of the
front door and shut it behind her. Lucky
looked at the now closed door and gave a
yap. **Lizzie had forgotten her!**

She gave another yap but Lizzie still didn't come back and Lizzie's mum and dad didn't even hear her.

*

Lucky waited for Lizzie by the front door all day long, except when she was eating her food in the kitchen with Lizzie's mum and dad or going out into the garden straight afterwards.

She was still waiting by the front door when Lizzie finally walked up the path that afternoon. The puppy was **SOOOOOO** happy she danced around with delight, her tail wagging nineteen to the dozen.

Lizzie threw her arms round the furry little body and hugged her close.

★

The next day when Lizzie went to school, Lucky still wanted to go with her. But she didn't yap when the door closed and she was left behind. The little dog waited by the front door on and off all day, going back and forth to check if Lizzie was coming home yet. But she also went to see what Lizzie's mum and dad were doing every now and again.

She was by the front door when she heard someone walking up the path and jumped up. Even though she knew it wasn't Lizzie, she was keen to investigate. Suddenly there was a **rattling**

outside the door and the next moment, a square piece of paper with something inside it came fluttering down on to the floor.

Lucky looked at the envelope on the mat and then at the flap it had come from. She tilted her head to one side, waiting for more envelopes to drop through, but they didn't and the footsteps on the path went away.

Lucky scraped at the envelope with her paws, then picked it up in her mouth and carried it into the kitchen where Lizzie's mum and dad were working on their laptops. They were very excited when they realized what the puppy had done. They kept raising their thumbs and smiling, and

Dad even gave her a tasty treat.

Lucky went back to the front door to
see if any more post had come through
the flap, but it hadn't. So she lay down
and closed her eyes, waiting for the sound
of Lizzie's footsteps.

★

When Lizzie came in, her parents couldn't wait to show her what Lucky had done.

'We didn't teach her,' Mum signed.

'Lucky taught herself,' signed Dad.

To demonstrate what he meant, Dad went out of the front door and posted an envelope back through the letterbox. Lucky picked it up and brought it over to a delighted Lizzie. She held up her thumbs and Lucky spun round in a small circle of joy.

She loved that sign!

★

A little while later, Lucky kept close to Lizzie as they headed over the road and in through Ted's side gate.

Lucky liked Ted very much, but she

was not at all sure about Ted's rats,
Gobbler and Jaws. She yapped at the
piping that ran round Ted's bedroom
as the rats raced along it, their claws
making little tapping sounds, before
sliding down into their cage.

Lucky looked up at Lizzie for
reassurance and whined. Lizzie
smiled and gave her furry head
a stroke. Lucky looked
back at the piping.

'Let's see if Lucky

likes Wriggles and Thumper,' signed
Ted, and Lizzie nodded. So off they
went outside.

As soon as Ruby the
cat spotted Lucky, she
hopped off the fence into
next-door's garden. The
puppy watched her go and gave a whine.

She was very excited to see Thumper
and Wriggles, though, wagging her tail
and wanting to play. The
rabbits weren't quite so sure.
Thumper **THUMPED**
one of his feet on
the floor of the
hutch; Wriggles hid behind
the willow twisted ball

they liked to chew on. Lucky sat down in front of the hutch, looked up at Lizzie and Ted, and back at the rabbits, then put out her paw.

The rabbits might not have wanted to play, but Victor did. He gave a **woof** from next door's garden and Lucky went racing over to the wire fence, tail wagging, to investigate.

Mrs Rose beckoned to Lizzie and Ted to come round.

Victor sniffed at Lucky's face and wagged his tail as soon as he saw her at the front door with Lizzie and Ted. Once Mrs Rose had given Lucky a friendly cuddle and a stroke, the two dogs trotted out into the back garden to play ball

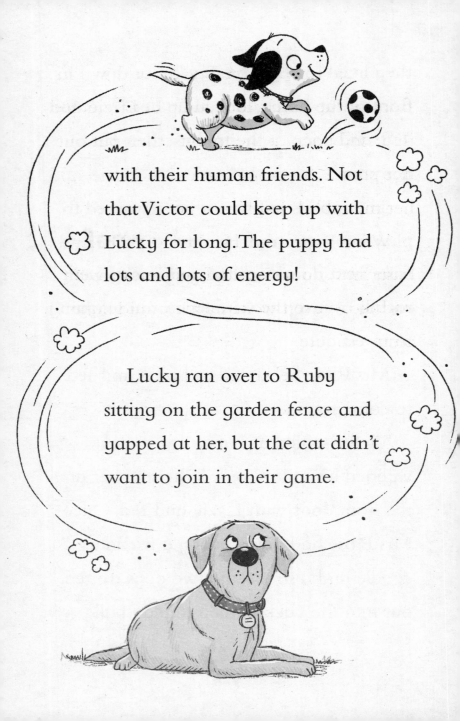

with their human friends. Not
that Victor could keep up with
Lucky for long. The puppy had
lots and lots of energy!

Lucky ran over to Ruby
sitting on the garden fence and
yapped at her, but the cat didn't
want to join in their game.

★

Back at her own home later, Lucky picked up more bits of paper and toys and clothes and shoes and brought them to Lizzie, and her mum and dad.

When it was time for bed, she'd been so busy that she was completely exhausted and didn't even wake up for a midnight play.

CHAPTER

On Saturday morning Lucky woke up
expecting this day to be just like all the
others had been since she'd first met Lizzie.
Lizzie would go off to school and Lucky
would wait for her by the front door, apart
from when she was eating, or bringing in
the post, or alerting everyone to the fact
that the doorbell had rung.

But on Saturday Lizzie didn't go to
school. She clipped Lucky's lead to her
collar, which the puppy was still getting

used to, and they set off for the castle ruins to pick some more tasty grass in the wildflower meadow for Wriggles and Thumper.

When they got there, Lizzie let the puppy off the lead so she could sniff about while Lizzie knelt down to pick some grass and put it in her *Animal Rescue* tote bag.

There were lots of butterflies visiting the wildflowers and Lucky went to say hello to one and then another, but they always flew away when she got too close. Lucky wasn't deterred, though, and just wagged her tail as she bounced off towards the next potential friend.

But all of a sudden, she heard the **rattle and rumble** of a van heading down the road towards them. Lucky stopped dead for a moment before running over to Lizzie, who was still kneeling in the grass.

Lizzie stroked the puppy, her face frowning. What was wrong? Trembling with fear, Lucky looked over in the direction of the road and Lizzie followed her gaze. Fortunately, they were hidden from view by the long grass and wildflowers, but they were able to see what was happening from their vantage point.

Lizzie gasped when she spotted the familiar white van

approaching them. It had the same number plate as the one Lucky had been in. Or at least the first part of it was the same – she couldn't see the last bit because it was covered in mud.

Once the van had driven past, Lizzie stood up. She watched carefully as it headed down the road and then turned into one of the smaller side streets. Lizzie quickly clipped on Lucky's lead and they ran after it.

A few minutes later, they turned the corner and Lizzie hastily pulled Lucky behind a bush. The van was just ahead of them – parked across the driveway of a run-down building. The man who'd stolen Lucky was pulling a big black plastic sheet over the top of it. That's why it hadn't been found before.

IT HAD BEEN HIDDEN!

Once the van was completely covered, the man went into the house and Lizzie and the puppy crept closer. Lucky could smell and hear the dogs whining and barking inside the garage even if Lizzie couldn't.

Lizzie quickly took a photo of the

covered-up van and then they went back to their hiding place behind the bush. She pulled out her phone and texted

Dog thief

to the police, along with the number plate and the name of the road where the van was parked.

A few minutes later, two police cars came **hurtling** round the corner. They pulled up on to the driveway, making sure that the van wasn't going anywhere. Then the police strode up to the house and knocked on the door.

Lizzie didn't hear the man shouting when he opened the door, but she could

tell he was because of his angry face, snarling mouth and the way his arms were moving.

As she watched the police questioning him, she saw the man pull a set of keys from his pocket and throw them down a drain before they could stop him. Then the officers put handcuffs on the man and led

him over to one of the police cars. Lizzie
saw them put him into the back of the
vehicle and shut the door while one of the
officers stood guard.

A moment later, Mary drove up and
Lizzie and the puppy ran over to her.

'You found the van?' Mary asked as
Lizzie lip-read her and nodded. She made
the sign for 'both of us' because Lucky had
helped too.

It took the police less than six seconds
to break open the garage door and reveal
what was inside. Mary looked dismayed,
Lucky whimpered and Lizzie's mouth fell
open at the sight of the stolen dogs in
cages stacked on top of each other.

Soon after that, more animal welfare

vehicles arrived and people got out to help.

'Thank you,' Mary signed to Lizzie as she and her staff headed inside the garage to take the stolen dogs to the animal shelter and safety.

When Lizzie and Lucky got home, Lizzie told her parents what had happened and what they'd seen. Lizzie signed to her dad that the one-hundred-and-first reason to have a dog was because it could help to catch a dog thief!

Her dad signed back that they only needed one reason to have Lucky – **because they loved her.** Lucky wagged her tail in agreement.

CHAPTER 15

A week later, Lucky was waiting by the front door for Lizzie to come home from school when a letter dropped through the letterbox. It was thicker and smaller than usual, and easier to scrape up with her paws. The puppy trotted into the kitchen with the letter in her mouth.

Usually Lizzie's mum and dad opened the post she brought them straight away, but not this time. Instead, they looked at each other, smiled and left it on the

counter. Lucky waited expectantly for
Dad to get her a tasty ***thank you for
bringing in the post*** treat.

★

When Lizzie came home from school,
Lucky was waiting for her as always.
Lizzie stroked the puppy and Lucky
wagged her tail. At last her friend was
home and it was time for fun to begin.

Lucky followed Lizzie into the kitchen
where Mum and Dad pointed to the
envelope on the counter.

Lizzie frowned as she picked it up and
opened it. Then she looked at her parents,
grinned, and made the sign for 'invitation'
and 'everyone'. Lucky knew something
good was happening by their happy faces

and gestures. She gazed at each of them in turn, wagging her tail. Then she ran to find the four-legged octopus tug toy and came running over to Lizzie with it for a play.

★

A few weeks after that, Lizzie was given the **Young Person's Animal Rescue Award** for spotting the dog thief's van and reporting him. There was a special ceremony at the animal rescue centre and Lizzie, Lucky, Mum and Dad were invited to attend.

Lizzie's hearing aids were decorated with paw prints for the occasion. Her mum and dad were wearing spotty Dalmatian-inspired outfits.

'**Exciting!**' signed Mum and Dad when they got there.

Lizzie's knees were shaking like leaves as she and Lucky went up on to the stage, but the puppy wasn't scared one bit and wagged her tail at everyone sitting in their seats watching them.

Lizzie's mum and dad waved their hands in the air instead of clapping so she could see how proud they were of her. The other people around them, and soon the entire audience, stopped clapping and started jazz-handsing too.

Lizzie signed 'thank you', her face beaming. Then she signed that Lucky helped her and should have a reward too, so Mary came out with another medal for the puppy.

'You **both** deserve these awards,' she said. 'Without your combined efforts, I dread to think what would have happened. Those poor dogs thank you as well – you saved them.'

★

Back at home there was a surprise party to celebrate. Ted, his gran, Mrs Rose and Victor were there, and so were Mrs Samuels, Molly and one of Lucky's brothers and two of her sisters!

Lucky brought over the four-legged octopus tug toy so they could all have a play with it.

'I'm glad she likes it so much,' Mrs Rose smiled.

Ted had drawn up a list specially for the occasion and stuck it on the wall. It showed ten reasons why Lizzie and Lucky were great **PET DETECTIVES**, and made Lizzie think that she'd like to solve more pet-related mysteries in the future.

Next to this, Dad had stuck Lizzie's list:

101 REASONS WHY
HAVING A DOG WOULD BE
A REALLY, REALLY,
REALLY GOOD IDEA.

Then the doorbell rang and Lucky ran
to greet Mary from the animal rescue
centre, who was accompanied by the
elderly Cavalier King Charles spaniel
from the thief's garage.

Lucky made a happy sound as the
two dogs nuzzled each other's faces,
their tails wagging.

'Daisy lives just down the street from you, so I thought we'd knock and say hello on her way home,' Mary said, as Lizzie lip-read. 'She's been having treatment at the centre.'

Lizzie kneeled down to stroke the gentle old dog that Lucky was so obviously fond of.

'I expect Daisy's owner will want to come and thank you for helping to get her back. I know I would. You two did some fantastic detective work,' Mary said.

Lucky put out her paw to Daisy and wagged her tail. She whined and tried to follow as Mary led her away. Daisy looked back at her friend.

'See you soon, Daisy,' Lizzie waved.

She stroked Lucky and Lucky looked up at her and wagged her tail.

'LIZZIE AND LUCKY: Pet Detectives and Mystery Solvers'

Lizzie signed to her pet, smiling as they headed back inside to join the party. 'I wonder what our next mystery will be?'

THE END

THANK YOU

This has been one of my absolute favourite books to write and I do hope you enjoy reading it too. I love the illustrations that Tim Budgen has done – the characters just seem to jump off the page. I wear hearing aids like Lizzie and love the decorations on hers. Thank you, Tim and also to designers, Arabella Jones and Mandy Norman.

When I was a child, we didn't learn sign language at my school. I wish I'd learned it then but it's never too late. Now I know lots and am learning more all the time. My sign language tutor for Levels 2 and 3 has been Jagjeet Rose. Jagjeet is always really helpful and makes learning lots of fun. I love using sign language to chat to my friends. Maybe one day I'll even have a sign language chat with you!

My two editors, Emma Jones and Sara Jafari, always make my job as a children's author an absolute pleasure. Thank you.

Other people who have helped to make this book happen are my sensitivity readers Gift Ajimokun and Guntaas Chugh, copy-editors Mary O'Riordan, Pippa Shaw and Stephanie Barrett, and proofreaders Leah Boulton and Bea McIntyre. I was really excited to work with Pippa because she knows sign language too! And Steph's got two new kittens called Pretzel and Flapjack, who love chewing the corners of books — so lucky!

I'm so looking forward to working with

my new publicist, Phoebe Williams, and marketer, Michelle Nathan, but will miss Louise Dickie – and her treacle flapjacks!

Thank you very much to Rozzie Todd, Toni Budden and Kat Baker for working so hard on the sales side of things.

The Society of Authors have been really supportive right from the start of my career. As has my lovely agent Clare Pearson.

My husband Eric's favourite BSL sign is 'meerkat'. My favourite one is 'turtle' – and also 'dogs', of course! My two dogs, Freya and Ellie, both know some signs – but not as many as Victor the hearing dog, inspired by real-life Victor.

Thanks to everyone who helped create this book and, most of all, thank you to you for reading it!

LEARN TO SIGN

**Can you read the dedication at the front
of the book using sign language?**

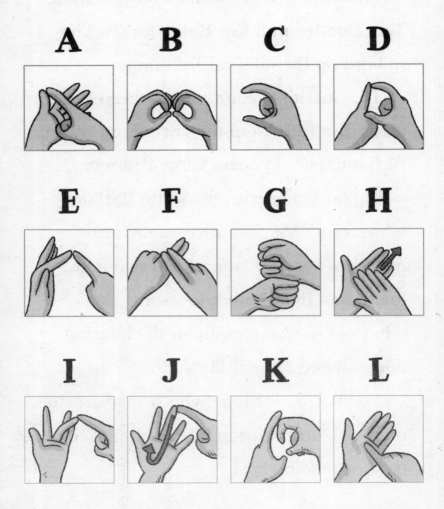

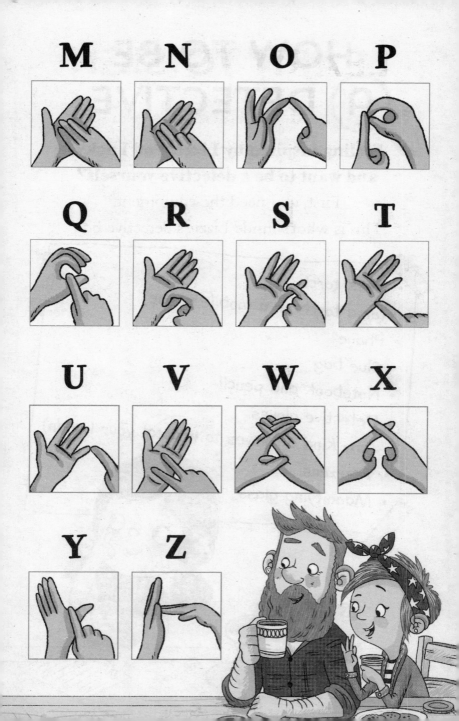

HOW TO BE  DETECTIVE

Feeling inspired by Lizzie and Lucky, and want to be a detective yourself?

First, you need the equipment.

This is what's inside Lizzie's detective bag:

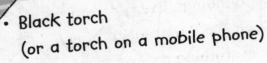

- Black torch
  (or a torch on a mobile phone)
- Phone
- Clue bag
- Notebook and pencil
- Detective gloves
  (any kind of gloves to protect your hands)
- Tweezers
- Magnifying glass

Next, you need to dress the part.
Wear clothes that help you blend in – plain clothes would work well!

Then, in your notebook, begin writing things you notice about your surroundings. Every detective has a keen eye – that means they observe everything around them. Maybe look outside your window and note down everything you see.

You can use your torch to inspect dark areas, perhaps under the sofa or your bed – you never know what you might find! If you see anything suspicious, use your tweezers to carefully pick it up and put it inside your clue bag.

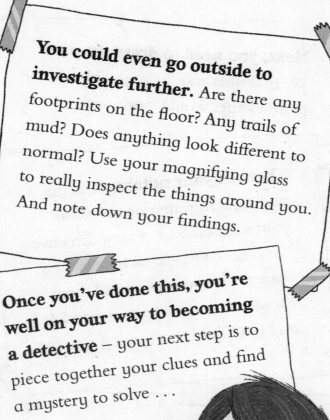

You could even go outside to investigate further. Are there any footprints on the floor? Any trails of mud? Does anything look different to normal? Use your magnifying glass to really inspect the things around you. And note down your findings.

Once you've done this, you're well on your way to becoming a detective – your next step is to piece together your clues and find a mystery to solve . . .